CHOOSE YOUR OW

MW01054611

Kids Love *Choose Your Own Adventure*®!

I love that I can choose if sometimes I want to take a risk or sometimes want to be safe. *Choose Your Own Adventure*s are different than regular books. Sometimes the safer choice is actually the more dangerous choice.
Fiona Wanner, age 8

You can read the same books over and over, but each time, it's a different adventure.
Sheldon Frank, age 8

An awesome adventure. Of course I'd do it again!
Manny Van Fleet, age 8

The adventures are really cool. Each adventure can be an adventure for you, but you are reading a book.
Rebecca Frank, age 8

Illustrated by Norm Grock
Book design by Stacey Boyd, Big Eyedea Visual Design
For information regarding permission, write to:

CHOOSECO
P.O. Box 46
Waitsfield, Vermont 05673
www.cyoa.com

A DRAGONLARK BOOK

Publisher's Cataloging-In-Publication Data
(Prepared by The Donohue Group, Inc.)

Names: Preller, James, author. | Grock, Norm, illustrator.
Title: Fairy house / by James Preller ; illustrated by Norm Grock.
Other Titles: Choose your own adventure. Dragonlarks.
Description: Waitsfield, Vermont : Chooseco, [2022] | Series: Choose your own adventure | Series: A Dragonlark book | Interest age level: 005-008. | Summary: "Bored at home and ignored by your workaholic parents, you decide to go outside and build a fairy house, and just when you're sure nothing is going to happen, you meet Bert the Below Average: a real, live fairy. He's not exactly what you had in mind, but he'll do. Let the adventure begin!"-- Provided by publisher.
Identifiers: ISBN 9781954232051 (paperback)
Subjects: LCSH: Fairies--Juvenile fiction. | Dwellings--Juvenile fiction. | CYAC: Fairies--Fiction. | Dwellings--Fiction. | LCGFT: Fantasy fiction. | Action and adventure fiction. | Choose-your-own stories.
Classification: LCC PZ7.P915 Fa 2022 | DDC [E]--dc23

Published simultaneously in the United States and Canada

Printed in China
12 11 10 9 8 7 6 5 4 3

CHOOSE YOUR OWN ADVENTURE®

Fairy House

BY JAMES PRELLER

ILLUSTRATED BY NORM GROCK

A DRAGONLARK BOOK

For Cavan & Clare,
my friends across the street.
I hope that my tree fairy
visits your house someday!
— JP

READ THIS FIRST!!!

WATCH OUT!
THIS BOOK IS DIFFERENT
from every book you've ever read.

Do not read this book from the first page
through to the last page.
Instead, start on page 1 and read until you
come to your first choice. Then turn to the
page shown and see what happens.

When you come to the end of a story,
you can go back and start again.
Every choice leads to a new adventure.

Good luck!

You sit on a tire swing in your backyard. Kicking the air, going nowhere. Bored, bored, bored. Your parents work at home and stare at their computers all day long. You feel lonely and there's nothing to do. But you remember something your grandmother once said: "If you build a wee home with love and care, a magic fairy will come. It only takes faith and a little imagination."

Could it be true? You decide to find out.

You pick a spot beneath an oak tree. You gather up acorns, tree bark, pine cones, a cardinal feather, flower petals, stones, and more. You make a little bed of sticks, cushioned with soft fir needles. You add a layer of moss for a blanket. You finish it all off with two magnolia leaves framing the front door.

Turn to the next page.

2

Your fairy home looks awesome—a magical little world—and you want to show someone.

"Maybe later," your mother says, click-clacking on the computer keyboard.

"Maybe later," your father says, scrolling through rows of numbers on the computer screen.

Neither parent even looks at you.

The black cat, Midnight, seems curious. She follows you outside, prowling softly on padded feet.

And you wait, and you wait some more. But nothing happens—because nothing ever does. Oh well. You set up your stuffed bunny, Old Mister Ears, to keep watch. You go inside for the night.

Turn to page 5.

The next morning, you check. Strange, the moss blanket has been tossed to the ground. Perhaps it was the wind. Or a restless chipmunk. An acorn falls, landing with a dull thump. You hear a groan: "Oof!" You see a flash of movement, quick as a hummingbird. But it wasn't that. These wings *glowed*.

You spring to your feet to investigate. Moving quickly, you peek around the old oak to gaze at the quivering stems of April daffodils. Something cowers behind them.

You drop to your hands and knees, scarcely breathing.

Hardly taller than your thumb, the creature has unusually large eyes, long skinny legs, and the small, delicate wings of a honeybee.

And so you say, ever so gently, "Well, hello there."

Turn to the next page.

The fairy—it could only be a fairy, nothing else— peeks around his closed fingers. Spiky blue hair pokes out from the top of his skull. His ears are pointy. His knees tremble in fear. And he gasps at the sight of your enormous head and very large nose.

You whisper, "Don't be afraid, I won't hurt you."

The little fellow's wings flutter, lifting his feet off the ground. He moves toward you. "My, you are a frightful thing, aren't you? What a great honking nose you have! Enormous!"

You touch your nose. "It's not that big."

"Terrifically ugly—you are, you are!" the garden fairy exclaims. "I surely would not want to be around when you sneeze out of that monstrosity. I say—that's it!" he snaps his fingers. "You must be a HUMAN BEAN!"

"A *being*," you reply. "A human being. Not a bean."

The fairy waves a hand. "Whatever."

Go on to the next page.

You ask, "What's your name?"

The fairy stares at his feet for a long moment. "I am known as . . . BERT THE BELOW AVERAGE!"

You try not to laugh.

"What's the matter? Don't you like my name?" he asks.

"Oh, Bert the Below Average is a fine name," you reply. "It's just that I thought you'd have a more, oh, *special* sort of name."

Bert's wings sag the way a dog's tail might fall between its legs when it is sad or anxious. "Oh, I know," Bert retorts. "You hoped for something fancy like, let me guess, Silverwings or Emerald Dancer or Bert the Rather Decent? Is that it?"

"I suppose," you admit. "I'm sorry, Bert. It *is* a very fine name. Strong and powerful. Bert the Below Average! A name for kings and . . . whatever it is *exactly* that you are."

Bert stands a little taller, both hands folded across his chest. "I am Bert Jansen. Your temporary, fill-in, replacement, part-time garden fairy."

Turn to the next page.

"MEOW!"
Your cat, Midnight, suddenly appears. She hisses and arches her back, ready to attack.

"ACK! A tiger!" Bert cries.
He raises a wand and points it at your cat.

If you swoop up the cat in your arms,
turn to the next page.

If you push Bert out of the way,
turn to page 16.

You snatch up Midnight the cat, holding her close.

"A beastie! A terrible, horrible beastie!" Bert squeals. "Get out of the way, Human Bean! I will turn the terrible, horrible beastie into . . . into . . . into a chocolate ice cream cone!"

Go on to the next page.

"Oh, Bert, you are a brave one," you say. "But this is only my sweet cat, Midnight. She is a kind creature—except to mice. Perhaps she thought you were a mouse?"

"A mouse? What an insult! Take it away this instant!" Bert demands. He waves his wand. "Or I'll turn it into a teapot!"

"You'll do no such thing," you say.

Midnight purrs in your arms.

Bert thinks for a moment. He says, "I'll grant you a wish if you promise to take the horrible beastie far away."

If you decide to ask for a wish,
turn to the next page.

If you prefer to think more carefully about it,
turn to page 13.

"Oh, yes, please!" You point to your stuffed bunny, slumped against the tree. "I wish for my favorite toy, Old Mister Ears, to come alive!"

"Okay, sure," Bert says. "That would be— hmm—let me see if I remember this correctly—"

"Oh, hurry, please," you insist.

"Are you absolutely positively sure?" Bert warns. "Wishes do not come with guarantees. I have been known to make mistakes."

If you trust Bert, turn to page 14.

If you are still a bit worried, turn to page 31.

You decide that you need time to think about this.

You ask, "What do you mean, 'temporary, fill-in, replacement, part-time' garden fairy?"

"I'm not—exactly—official," Bert admits.

"Well, are you a magic fairy?"

Bert shakes his head no, but answers: "Sort of."

"Sort of?" you repeat, hands on your hips. "Can you do magic . . . or not?"

Bert sprinkles magic dust into the air. He chants, "Ala boo, ala bee, ala you, ala me. Let's see!"

If you believe in Bert's magic, turn to page 35.

If you aren't convinced Bert has magic, turn to page 37.

You answer, "Please, yes! Make Old Mister Ears come alive!"

"I hope this works," Bert says. He crosses his fingers. "Not like last time."

"Wait, what do you mean, 'last time'? I thought you knew how to grant wishes!"

"I told you," Bert replies. "I *do* make mistakes. I'm not usually sent on these errands. I work behind the scenes. Support staff. Odds and ends, bits and bats. But these are trying times, as you know. Fairy house construction is way up. We've had to get creative in order to meet demand."

"What do you usually do?" you ask.

"I fix and mend things. Toasters are my specialty." Bert says the word with a great flourish, so that it sounds like this: spee-SHE-ali-TEEEEE. He looks around. A worm crawls nearby. Bert wriggles his nose with displeasure. "This is not my usual . . . assignment."

Turn to page 24.

The wee fairy raises his wand. His face looks angry. Desperate to save your cat, you push Bert out of the way. Sparks fly. The fairy tumbles to the ground. Midnight scampers to safety.

"I'm awfully sorry," you say. "But I was afraid you were going to hurt my cat."

"Dirt!" the fairy cries. "Dirt on my knees! Horror of horrors! Rats and snails and garbage pails! Now I'm very upset."

You explain, "I had to do something."

Bert the Below Average grumbles. "Oh, it's my fault. I ruin everything. I'm a magic fairy who can't do anything right."

"Oh?"

"Watch and see for yourself." Bert points at a passing car. "Walla zip, walla zing—ice cream bell, ring a ding-ding!"

Turn to page 18.

ZAP! BRINNNNG! The car turns into an ice cream truck!

"Yum!" you cry.

You race to the ice cream truck. But the man in the truck frowns at you. "We only have three flavors—spinach, broccoli, or liverwurst."

You decide that you aren't very hungry after all.

Back in your yard, you complain to Bert.

"What kind of fairy are you? Liverwurst ice cream? That's gross!"

Bert shrugs and says, "That's why they call me Bert the Below Average, not Bert the Very Good."

But it gives you an idea. Maybe you could help Bert be a better fairy. And then you get a mischievous idea: *or* you could capture him and show the world that you found a magic fairy!

If you decide to try to capture Bert, turn to the next page.

If you decide to try to help the magic fairy, turn to page 51.

You lunge forward, hoping to snatch the little man in your hands. After all, no one has *ever* brought a magic fairy into school! It might help you make new friends.

Zip, zap, zup. Bert easily darts away.

He buzzes by your ear.

"Oh, that was a mistake, my friend," he says in a singsong voice. "A lesson you must be taught. Oh yes! I shall turn you into a . . ."

You cry out, "NO!"

But with a wave of his wand and a sprinkle of dust, you are suddenly turned into an inchworm . . . sitting on a leaf . . . high up in the tree.

"HELP ME!" you cry.

But your voice is too small for anyone to hear.

A bird lands on a nearby branch.

It is a bluebird, with hungry babies to feed back at the nest. It inspects you closely.

Oh no, you think. *This can't be good.*

Maybe Bert will turn you back?

The End

"You can do it, Bert," you say. "Bring Old Mister Ears to life! It's my wish."

Old Mister Ears stares at you for a long moment. His eyes narrow. Smoke leaks from his nose. He grows bigger, stronger, and a lot scarier.

"Oh, dear," Bert murmurs.

"Mister Ears?" you say.

Your plush bunny opens its mouth . . . and out shoots a stream of fire!

You jump and tumble out of the way. "Bert, you turned my best friend into a fire-breathing dragon!"

"Yeah, sorry about that," Bert replies. "Nobody's perfect."

"ROAWWWWWRRR!" Old Mister Ears roars.

"I have an idea!" you cry. "S'mores!"

You run inside for marshmallows, graham crackers, and chocolate.

Turn to page 25.

"Hmm," you say. You thought you were making a house for a garden fairy. You've never heard of a TOASTER fairy.

But after a pause, you shrug. "I trust you, Bert. Let's do this! Besides, he's just a fuzzy old bunny. What can possibly go wrong?"

"Oh, you'd be surprised," Bert replies.

*If you encourage Bert to try,
turn to page 22.*

*If you change your wish to one
that's out of this world,
turn to page 45.*

"Nice and toasty," Bert says, as you roast marshmallow after marshmallow on the dragon's fire. He shoves another s'more into his mouth. But soon you are out of marshmallows. And the dragon is looking at you . . . kind of funny.

But not "ha-ha" funny.

It's more of an "oh-no" funny.

Yipes.

"It's time for a dragon battle," Bert tells you. "You know that, right?"

If you run away, turn to page 27.

If you stay to battle the dragon, turn to page 41.

"RUN AWAY!" Bert yells.

Old Mister Ears roars again.

Quickly, you duck behind a bush. "Do something, Bert!"

Bert sighs. He slumps his shoulders. And groans. "Why must it always be *me* who does something?"

"You turned my bunny into a dragon—that's why!" you scream.

"Oh, well, if you put it that way," Bert says.

He flutters his wings, sprinkles some dust, and says, "Dragon no, bunny yes, if this works—it's anybody's guess!"

There's a flash of light.

Turn to the next page.

You look—and Old Mister Ears is gone!

In his place, there's a snuggly, cuddly, very real puppy.

"Meow."

"Meow?" You look at Bert. "Seriously?"

Bert shrugs. "Hey, nobody's perfect."

You pick up the puppy, snuggle it close. "Is that you, Mister Ears?"

The puppy licks your face.

"Thank you," you say to Bert. "I'm very happy."

"And so my work is done," Bert says. In that instant, Bert's hair turns from blue to a bright, shining silver—and he vanishes into air.

The End

You start to have doubts about your magic fairy.

"If you aren't sure . . ." you start to say to Bert.

Suddenly, a bubble of light drifts down from the sky and interrupts you. It flashes brightly and three colorful fairies—Pink, and Emerald, and Blue—twinkle before you.

"Uh-oh," Bert groans. "Here comes the Doom Squad."

"Tsk, tsk, tsk," the Pink Fairy says. "Oh, Bert. What have you done now?"

"We've been through this foolishness before, Bert," the Emerald Fairy scolds. "Get back to Fairyland. We'll deal with you later."

Bert hangs his head, snaps his fingers . . . and disappears.

You stand there, confused—and amazed. "Can somebody please tell me what's going on?"

"We are frightfully sorry," the Blue Fairy says. Her wings sparkle in the sunlight. "This has been a terrible mistake."

Turn to the next page.

"Bert is not always a 'good' fairy," the Pink Fairy explains, making quote marks with her delicate fingers at the word *good*. "He likes to play tricks."

"He's naughty," the Emerald Fairy says, giggling.

"So what now?" you wonder.

"We bid you goodbye," the Blue Fairy says.

"But what about my wish?"

The three fairies giggle. "Oh, dear, no! A wish? Like a genie in a bottle, from a children's storybook? Or a magic fish? Oh, that is too funny!"

"I don't get it," you say, offended.

The Blue Fairy sees that you are unhappy. "We *would* if we *could*," she explains. "But fairy magic doesn't work that way. We don't perform tricks like trained seals."

"Oh, no," the Pink Fairy says. "We are *not* seals."

"We are magical *beings*—not magicians," the Emerald Fairy concludes.

Go on to the next page.

And with that, they vanish into air, leaving behind not even the tiniest sprinkle of fairy dust.

You climb onto the tire swing. You kick the air, going nowhere. Another dull day. And you are bored, bored, bored.

The End

You believe in Bert's magic. He's a fairy, anyone can see that!

"Whoa!" you exclaim. "I'm shrinking! This is amazing!"

Your body gets smaller and smaller—as everything around you grows bigger and bigger.

A mushroom towers over your head.

Blades of grass stand like tall pines.

You are not much taller than an ant.

That's when you see the gigantic spider coming toward you.

If you decide to hide,
turn to page 38.

If you decide to stand and fight the spider,
turn to page 39.

"I don't believe in your magic!" you say to Bert.

"Well, you'd better, because it's real—although I think I may have said that spell, uh, TERRIBLY wrong," says Bert.

"WAIT!" you cry.

But it's too late. You've been turned into a statue. Solid stone.

"Rats and snails!" Bert exclaims. "I hate when that happens."

And so, on silver wings, he flitters away.

You watch him go. It begins to rain. The water runs down your face like tears. You wish for an umbrella. But none of your wishes come true.

For, alas, you have been turned to stone.

The End

Thinking quickly, you press yourself against the far side of the mushroom.

"Oh, Bert!" you whisper. "I need your help, buddy!"

The spider marches toward you. STOMP, STOMP, STOMP, his eight legs hit the ground near you.

Your knees tremble.

POOF!

Bert appears beside you. "You called?"

"Thank goodness," you cry. "Hurry, quick. Save me from that terrible spider!"

"Spider? Did you say spider? Yipes! Eek! I'm afraid of spiders!" Bert turns to face the deadly creature . . . and faints.

"Bert!" you cry. You cower in fear. Suddenly, Bert is gone, the spider is gone, and you're in your own bed. What happened? You may never know.

The good news? It was a very exciting day!

The End

You pick up a stick.

The spider crawls toward you.

You slash and stab and swing the stick. *Whack*, you land a blow against the spider's abdomen. It backs away, injured.

Yes, victory!

You look up . . . in time to see a big owl flying above you.

*If you decide to leap out of the way,
turn to page 58.*

*If you speak to the owl,
turn to page 62.*

"You must battle!" Bert yells. "No magic can stop this monster!"

You watch as your garden fairy skitters away in fright. Gone, goodbye. He's left you alone.

You turn to look at Old Mister Ears.

His eyes are blazing yellow. He sniffs and coughs. Smoke pours from his ears.

Thinking quickly, you pull a mint from your pocket. You hold it out and say, "Here, Old Mister Ears. This cool mint will help with your scratchy throat."

Old Mister Ears looks at you, sniffling and blinking. He bends close and eats the mint from your hand.

Turn to the next page.

"YUM!" says Old Mister Ears, chomping your mint.

Old Mister Ears returns to his normal size and shape.

Except that he's not a stuffed rabbit anymore. He's alive. He's your real live friend.

Your time together will never be the same again. It will be better.

"Have you ever eaten a pancake with maple syrup?" you ask Old Mister Ears.

He wrinkles his bunny nose. No, he hasn't.

"Wait here," you say. "You're going to love it!"

The End

You close your eyes and make a new wish.

When they open, you are sitting on the moon with Old Mister Ears beside you.

The stars shine brightly in the black sky, nearer than ever before.

In the distance, an alien spaceship comes your way.

There are no words for the feelings that bubble up inside you. Old Mister Ears opens his arms and you hug each other warmly.

"I'm alive," he says, amazed.

"It was my deepest wish," you explain.

"Mine, too," he replies.

Bert sniffles behind you. He is crying, rubbing his eyes, blowing his nose. "Beautiful," Bert says between sobs. And he pronounces it "BEE-you-TEA-full!"

You say, "Oh, Bert! How can I ever thank you?"

Turn to the next page.

"Well, now that you mention it," Bert says, licking his lips. "Is there any chance I might try something the human beans call a CHOCOLATE CHIP? Two would be nice. Twenty-seven would be better! I hear they are delicious!"

"I'll bring three," you decide. "More than that, and you'll get a tummy ache. But there's just one problem."

"What's that?"

"We're on the moon—and those dudes don't look too friendly."

The alien spaceship has landed with you on the moon. Two aliens walk up to you, holding laser guns.

They don't look very nice.

Bert smiles, sprinkles some dust, and *whoosh*— you are back in your yard again.

"So cool!" You high-five with Old Mister Ears.

Go on to the next page.

"Just wait here, Bert. You're going to love chocolate chips."

You run inside and come back, lickity split.

Bert gladly gobbles up all three chips. *Yum!* He takes a small bow. "Now I must leave. There are other boys and girls for me to visit. Fairy houses are going up everywhere, it seems. My next stop is Dublin, Ohio!"

Turn to the next page.

"I thought you only mended toasters," you say.

"I've been promoted," Bert says, blushing. "It seems there's a great demand for magic fairies these days."

Before Bert goes away, you ask for one last wish.

Bert smiles and shakes his head. "Have you learned nothing yet? The magic is inside you. You've had it all along—that's why you could see me from the beginning."

Bert glances at kindly Old Mister Ears—and then he looks directly into your eyes. He says:

"*You have always had the power to make your own wishes come true.*"

Go on to the next page.

Then Bert closes his eyes, spreads his wings, and begins to glow. His entire body seems to hum a rich golden tone. The light grows brighter and brighter, until you have to look away.

And then it is over.

"What now?" wonders Old Mister Ears.

If you wish for an adventure in the water, turn to page 56.

If you wish for more friends for Old Mister Ears, turn to page 66.

"Maybe you need more practice," you suggest to Bert. Practice is how you learned how to tie your shoes, and ride a bike, and everything hard you've ever learned to do.

"Practice?"

"Yes, with your magic."

Bert smiles. He points his wand. "For a minute, for an hour—I turn you into a flower!"

ZAP, ZING!

And just like that, Bert the Below Average has turned you into a yellow daffodil.

So you wait, and you wait. A butterfly flutters by to say hello. A ladybug sits on your petals. After an hour, *whoosh*, you are back!

"Well done!" you tell Bert. "That was lovely!"

"I deserve a reward," Bert demands. "Hurry now, Human Bean. Bring me a treat from your Human Bean kitchen!"

---

*If you decide to give him a treat,
turn to the next page.*

If you say you won't, turn to page 54.

You run inside and return with a marshmallow. It is the size of Bert's entire body.

Bert pokes it with a finger. He flutters around the marshmallow, studying it. Finally, he tastes it—head first!—and smiles.

"Oh, glorious!" he cries. "Stupendous! Oh, joy! And for this, you can receive one wish."

Go on to the next page.

You think about it for a minute. Then you say, "I wish to ride a purple unicorn over a rainbow!"

"Ah, yes, well," Bert says. He rubs his hands together. "I shall do my best. A little of this, a little of that. Tick, tock, tick—I sure hope this does the trick!"

POOF!

To ride the unicorn,
turn to page 69.

If you'd rather have a surprise,
turn to page 72.

You answer, "I'm sorry, but I can't give you a treat. It's bad for your teeth. First, I would like my wish. Can't fairies grant wishes?"

Bert crosses his arms over his belly. "Not without a treat, we can't. Please?"

"No."

"Pretty please!" he pleads.

"Stop asking," you reply.

Go on to the next page.

Bert drops to his knees. He whines, "Please, oh please, oh please, please, please!!!"

"ARGHH," you groan. "I really wish you'd stop asking—"

"Okay!" Bert replies.

And with a wink, and a grin, he vanishes into thin air.

Your wish, after all, has come true.

The End

"I wish for an adventure," you say. "A water adventure!"

WHOOSH!

A rainbow of water sprays off your water skis. A pod of dolphins swims alongside you. Old Mister Ears waves from the speedboat. Three fairies—Blue, and Pink, and Emerald—flutter around his head.

"I am so happy!" he cries.
Yes, you think, *I'm happy, too*!

The End

You leap . . . but the owl lifts you up from the ground.

The owl flies into the sky. Its great white wings beat ceaselessly against the wind.

The world grows smaller and smaller.

"Oh, how I wish I was home again," you cry. A single tear falls to the ground.

In a flash of fairy dust, the owl releases you from its grip.

You fall—spinning, tumbling, cartwheeling through the sky.

Aaaaahhhhhhhhh!

But you land, ever so softly, with a plop, beside the fairy house that you built in your own backyard.

Bert sits on a pine-cone chair, beaming a smile at you. "Nice of you to drop by," he jokes.

"Your hair," you say. "It's turned silver!"

"Yes," he says, proudly. "I'm now an official, full-time, genuine fairy."

Turn to page 60.

"Does this mean goodbye?" you ask.

"Never goodbye," Bert answers. "Forever hello! I will always be nearby. Don't you wish to swim with mermaids? Or ride together on magic elephants—they fly, you know."

"Let's do it!" you exclaim.

And you know what?

After a sprinkling of fairy dust, that's exactly what you do!

The End

"Um, no, that's not happening," the rhino replies. "No wings. Besides, I'm afraid of heights. What if we just roll in the mud and call it a day?"

You sigh.

"Fine!"

The End

"Hello, owl," you say to the beautiful bird.

"Hello, friend!" the owl says. "And hello, Bert!"

Bert and the owl are friends!

"Nice day for a bubble ride, what do you say?"

"Of course!" says Bert.

Suddenly, a rainbowy bubble surrounds you.

You hear Bert's voice in your ear. "Never fear, the magic of the fairies will protect you. Come, time for us to fly!"

Go on to the next page.

The bubble, blown by a breeze, slips softly into the sunlit sky.

You look down. Your home is far below. Bert beats his magical wings by your side. The owl looks around happily.

"Nice to rest my wings!" says the owl.

You ask, "Where are we going?"

"Fairyland!" Bert exclaims. "We're going to a party. I've been promoted!"

"Will you be a real fairy now?"

"Yes," Bert answers. "And soon I will be given my official fairy name. I won't be Bert the Below Average anymore."

Turn to the next page.

The bubble floats higher and higher. In the distance, upon the clouds, you see a shining palace with golden paths and flowing fountains. Fairyland!

"What will your new name be?" you ask. "Wait, let me guess. Golden Wings? Sparkle Toes? Braveheart?"

"Wrong, wrong, wrong," Bert says with a smile. His eyes twinkle with joy. "My new name will be . . . BERT THE PRETTY GOOD!"

The End

"I wish you had some more friends who are just like you, Old Mister Ears," you say. Then your mom and dad tell you it is time for bed.

It is dark. You turn on a flashlight and follow the beam of light across your room.

You see Old Mister Ears. He is joined by several other plush toy friends: Elephant, Monkey, and Silly Moose. They are sitting at a table, all very much alive. They wave to you, and invite you to come for sweet honey tea.

You smile and join them.

Just as you had always dreamed it would be.

The End

You find yourself sitting on top of a purple unicorn. It is the most beautiful animal you have ever seen. You can feel its power and magic through the tips of your fingers as you grasp its silky mane.

"To the rainbow!" you cry.

WHOOSH!

One flap of its majestic wings lifts you off the ground. The unicorn rises into the sky. You fly past marshmallow clouds and into a mist of cotton candy and sprinkles.

Turn to the next page.

Down below, you see a forest of chocolate trees, a grape soda river, and a jiggling hill of green jelly.

The unicorn's broad wings flap easily.

The magic fairy appears on your shoulder. "Well, howdy-do!" he says.

"Bert," you cry. "You did it! Your magic is real!"

"Yes, I guess it is!" Bert smiles. "Never forget. As long as you believe, anything is possible— even unicorns and chocolate trees—"

"—and little blue-haired fairies named Bert!"

The two of you laugh together as you soar over the rainbow to the next magical adventure.

The End

"Send me to a different surprise!" you yell to Bert. You don't want to admit it, but unicorns scare you a little.

You find yourself sitting on the back of a saggy rhinoceros. It is standing in the mud, chewing on a bush.

You cry out, "Wait a minute! You aren't anything magical!"

"Never said I was," the rhino replies. Nom, nom, nom. It keeps eating the bush.

"BERT!" you scream. "BERT!"

There is no answer.

"I do have a horn on my nose," the rhino points out.

"Yes, but—"

"And I am gray," the rhino says. "That's a little bit magical."

"Not even close," you reply, rather sharply.

"Picky, picky," the rhino mutters.

"Okay, fine. Let's fly over that rainbow, my magical gray rhino!"

Turn to page 61.

ABOUT THE ARTIST

Norm Grock has always loved to draw. His love of drawing took him to college where he earned a degree in graphic design. Upon graduation, he worked as a lead illustrator for fifteen years creating illustrations for children. He's a published illustrator of children's books, game art, and comic books. As a freelance artist, he has a background in sequential art, video games, and character design. He lives in the Pacific Northwest with his wife, raising their two sons.

ABOUT THE AUTHOR

James Preller is the author of many critically acclaimed books for children, including the popular Jigsaw Jones Mysteries series. Other books include the Scary Tales series, The Big Idea Gang series, as well as picture books (*All Welcome Here, A Pirate's Guide to First Grade*) and many stand-alone middle-grade novels (*The Courage Test, Bystander, Blood Mountain, Six Innings, Upstander*, and more). Four of his books have been named Junior Library Guild Selections and others have received various awards, including a YALSA, a Cybil, NY Public Library's Best Books for Reading and Sharing, an ALA Notable, and others. James lives in upstate New York. He blogs regularly at Jamespreller.com and enjoys visiting schools (in person or virtually) as a guest author, sharing his love of books. This book, *Fairy House*, represents his first experience writing a *Choose Your Own Adventure* book, a dream come true and a fascinating puzzle for a writer—and a reader!—to solve.

For games, activities, and other fun stuff, or to write to James, visit us online at CYOA.com